Millennial Ball
Vampire Erotic Story

Tiny Sparks

Santos takes Caterina to his cousin, Lord Barth's cave, when they both find out they have the same deadline. Neither of their mates are pregnant yet, and the Millennial ball is two weeks away.

Between laughter and excited chatter, their mothers arrive with advice. But is it too late?

The Ball is a horrendous affair that leaves Caterina and Michaela in tears. The human blood bags are creatures without emotion or fight left in them. Except for one.

Alexandre tastes one blood bag after the other and finds them off putting. Never in his entire existence has he ever not found a delicious human to suck from at the Millennial Ball, where the servers are allowed to be fucked and sucked. None of them appeal to him, until his nose catches a fragrance that makes his fangs ache and his cock hard.

Only problem is, she's on the auction block, and his brother's mate has chosen her.

Chapter 1 Alexandre

I drank from the neck of my blood bag thinking about the upcoming ball. Selene was so over the moon with the two couples, it was disgusting. Why would you want to drink from one person for the rest of your existence? You could drink from others, but they would never taste as good as the mate, or so I've been told.

"Alex, stop."

Distracted, I lifted my head to watch Mary approach. "What's your problem now?"

She didn't backpaddle, something I hated, but at the same time, admired about her. "You're at the point of draining your last blood bag. We're not allowed to get another before the ball." I looked at the pale face of the woman I'd been drinking from. Disgusted, I threw her to the ground.

"She's still breathing. Plus, we've got yours." Mary avoided my gaze.

"Again?" I threw my hands up when she nodded.

"I was so hungry, and his blood was flowing so smoothly." A dreamy expression crossed her face.

"I changed you nine years ago, you should know to control your thirst by now." I rubbed my face.

"Like you?" She giggled and ran off, knowing that I would have her by the throat if I wasn't so distracted.

"Brian, can you clean this up, please?" I pointed at the female blood bag.

"Of course, sir." The butler muttered something under his breath, and a fog surrounded the girl, before disappearing.

"Any ideas in regards to acquiring a new blood bag before the ball?"

"My daughter sucked hers dry again?" He raised an eyebrow.

"Yes." We couldn't drink from Brian. He was a warlock and Mary's father. Drinking from me and combined with his magic has extended his life.

"She's going to need to behave at the ball, or my grandmother will kill her." I sighed.

The warlock sighed and nodded. I'd changed his daughter not out of kindness, but because I wanted power and Brian offered that in return for her life.

"Selene is excited with all the mating going around, but I need to introduce Mary." Grandmother Selene, the demi-goddess creator of vampires, was draconian with pro-creation. Natural born vampires were favored over made. I hoped my brother and cousin Barth couldn't get their mates pregnant. That would make my night way better. And maybe they refused to change their mates without pregnancy. Selene's wrath was legendary, she'd kill them for sure. If she killed Santos, I'd be the heir. We only differed one year in age, but he thought himself superior, even living in the new world. Disgusting. Our parents applauded it, Selene definitely not.

I loved the old ways, blood straight from the vein, no hiding my true nature, and except for the blood moon ball, I could take whichever human I wanted for a blood bag, as long as it was kept alive for a year minimum.

Brian's daughter shouldn't be so special, but she had the rare ability to stay hidden unless she wanted to be noticed. Eavesdropping was her favorite thing. Maybe I should send her to check out the state of Barth's mate?

"Mary, get your ass over here." My voice boomed through the castle, which was empty except for the three of us. Or four if you counted the unconscious human.

"You yelled, master." The cheeky little twit curtseyed. Her pink dress was frilly and wide enough to hide the giant cat.

"Cat outside, now," I ground out. That beast was a menace.

"Princess is a leopard, not a cat." She pouted, but the cat's eyes bored into mine. I squinted and hissed, and 'princess' ducked behind the skirts.

"Don't be such a bully." Her arms were crossed, and I closed my eyes, hoping for some patience, which I didn't possess.

"If you get any juicy information from Barth's cave, I'll allow the cat to stay inside." She cheered, and I held my hand up. "If I see her once, I will give animal blood a try."

"I promise she'll be good!"

I waved her off, and she left, the leopard following closely.

Chapter 2 Louisa

The town was in uproar with the upcoming blood moon ball. I rolled my eyes at people prancing around, showing off their dresses and suits.

Don't they realise that no one knows what happens after the ball? You get to attend, but you never get to talk about it since those people just disappear. Never to be seen again.

"Louisa, would you please wash your hair." My mother was excited, sure I would be picked this year. Not because I was pretty or anything. I was pale, and as she so delicately likes to put it, fat.

I hurried to the back of the house to wash my hair in the cold water bucket she'd put there for me. Rubbing the soap in my hair worsened the knots. I sighed knowing the torture session that was to follow.

"Get over here." She pointed to a chair and pulled the comb through my ratty hair. She paid no attention to my squalls. The woman lived to torture me. I never combed my hair. No one cared, why should I bother?

"The royals will be here soon. Is she almost ready?" Father didn't acknowledge me.

"Once I get this rat's nest untangled, yes," mother grunted.

She must have pulled out enough hair to make a wig. I knew not to make a fuss. It would only end with a hidden bruise from either or both of them. My mind wandered to the forest. Just so I wouldn't hear their thoughts. It was an annoying mental illness I had. I heard people's thoughts, and I didn't want to know what happened in my parents' minds, ever. As a kid, I did, and it was ugly. I cried for weeks, but never told them why.

By the time I was fifteen, they tried to marry me off, but my looks weren't good enough, and without a dowry, no one wanted me. I didn't mind because what went on in those men's dirty minds was disgusting.

I was now eighteen and on my way to becoming a spinster. My parents wanted me out of the house, and their hope was set one hundred percent on the drafting for the ball.

"Well, I tried my best. It'll have to do." Mother sighed. Wow, thanks, woman. It almost made me want to be picked. But running away from town would be a better option.

I jumped when a trumpet announced the arrival of the royals.

"Every single man and woman between the ages of eighteen and thirty-five, present yourself in the square immediately." A booming voice echoed throughout our small town.

Chapter 3 Alexandre

I jumped as grandma Selene popped in out of nowhere. "Jeez, woman."

"Watch your tongue," Selene snapped.

"You scared the c.. hell out of me." I held my non-beating heart.

"I need your help with the drafting in your neighboring watering hole."

I raised an eyebrow at her description of the small town that set roots on my land a long time ago. They were fertile, and with some mental coaxing, I kept them busy. My blood supply was insured. Fingers crossed she didn't take too many youngsters for the auction block.

"Can I have a taste before you take them to your castle?" I tried and failed at making pleading puppy eyes at grandma Selene.

"Why?" Her eyes narrowed, and I knew I shouldn't tell her about Mary yet. Neither about the nearly empty blood bag recovering upstairs. Though she might have smelled it, she didn't mention it, and neither would I.

"To see if I should take a special interest in one." I checked my nails, studiously avoiding her too keen eyes.

"Okay, I'll allow it. But you can't take advantage before the bidding starts. You know the rules." She warned.

Stupid rules. I wanted fresh blood now. Out of the corner of my eyes I noticed Mary, and shook my head. She slid back into the shadows. Good girl. That was a close call.

I took a deep breath. "Right, when do we leave?" Before I finished the question, the bloody woman disappeared into thin air.

Grumbling under my breath, I shrouded myself and hurried to town.

Chapter 4 Louisa

We were lined up on the square like cattle, when a beautiful ageless woman appeared out of thin air, followed by a broody dark haired, leather clad, extremely handsome guy. My focus was off and all the thoughts floated into my brain. Swooning from the girls and disgusting remarks from the guys about the woman, which I'm sure she wouldn't appreciate.

Suddenly, only one voice remained: *"The smell of these desperate humans. Bleh, disgusting. I'd love for there to be a way to enjoy and smell the blood without their odor."*

Swiveling my head, I tried to find the person attached to the senseless thoughts. Blood bag? And what's with the human remarks? Maybe I was picking up on an animal's thoughts? It's not like it was the first time, but it hadn't been as clear as this.

"Thank you all for attending the selection. As you know, it's a great honor to be allowed at the castle during the ball," the woman droned on.

A great honor, my ass. I was pretty sure something bad went on in there, and the feeling worsened as I felt someones' gaze on me. The brooding guy raised an eyebrow. Jeez, creep, look at someone else, would you. I crossed my arms under my breasts.

"I would, if there was anyone else that held my interest even more than a second. I can't wait to taste your blood."

"Oh, gross." I gagged at the thought. Staring straight at him, I caught his eyes widening. *What's wrong with you? What other weird thoughts are you hiding?*

"Let's see." He tapped a finger to his lips. *"What would you do if you knew I was a vampire, here to take you away to drink your blood and bury my cock inside your hot pussy."*

My mind went completely blank for a minute. Was he answering my thoughts on purpose or was this a coincidence? I turned toward the woman, trying to empty my mind and block other people's thoughts.

"Hold out your index finger for inspection, please." The woman moved down the line, followed by the weirdo. She shook her head at some, who left the line, and the ones who stayed got their finger...sucked? Seriously? The guy grimaced every so often, after which that person was dismissed.

Chapter 5 Alexandre

This plump girl with the translucent skin was a sight to behold. She took my breath away for reasons unknown to me. I never looked at humans beyond their blood supply, so why did I glance her way more than once? Once in a while, when there wasn't a vampire around willing to fuck, I'd use them for that, but I tried to avoid that. It was way too easy to break their mind. A vampire's mind was more complex. During sex, I'd get frustrated with the human, since I had to hold back on my commands and had to bite them to finish.

This human, though, was different.

I thought she answered my thoughts, when she reacted to my assessment of her blood tasting. The closer I got to her down the line, the better she smelled. When I arrived at her finger, I gazed straight at her and bent over her finger.

Will you taste sweet or savory, I wonder?

"My finger will taste salty from all the sweating, weirdo." Her sugar sweet smile told me she didn't know I could hear her loud and clear.

I winked before I penetrated her delicate finger with my fang. She gasped. When I sucked, I pushed images of me sucking on her nipple instead of her finger. Her moan was loud and clear, and so were her thoughts. *"Goodness me, I can feel the suction straight to my core."* When she closed her eyes, I added an image of my finger entering her and my thumb rubbing her clit. Her moan almost got me purring in response.

"Alexandre, are you finished?" Selene interrupted me.

I stood. "Not even close," I growled at her. "But I'll soon have my second taste, and maybe this time, I'll make sure your 'core' won't miss out," I whispered in the girl's ear.

Her hiss and gasp followed me when I left.

She would be mine, I'd make sure of it.

"I most definitely won't be yours. What the hell is going on here? And how on Earth did he make me wet by sucking my fingers and pushing those images in my mind?"

You Will be Mine and I'll fuck your pussy while sucking your blood until you orgasm so much you'll faint. I pushed the thought into her mind.

Her outrageous squeal turned heads, but thankfully, Selene was already gone, and the guards appeared with the carriage to take the five chosen from my town to the castle.

Getting back into the castle was a relief. I needed to get my head around what just happened. But before I sat on my throne, Mary approached.

"Tell me," I commanded.

"Well, Santos's human is pregnant, and your parents are there, overjoyed." She rolled her eyes. "Barth decided to change his woman, but wants to wait until the last minute, which I guess is tomorrow." Mary petted her giant cat, not that invested in the conversation.

"That's all?" I gripped the arms of my throne, restraining myself from strangling her when she tapped her lip.

"Oh, yes. They mentioned you." Her eyes glistened with mischief.

"And?" I ground out between clenched teeth, the wood creaking under the force of my grip.

"Everyone agreed that it would be great if you found your own mate. They think it's a shame it hasn't happened yet and that it might temper your aggression."

"I'm not aggressive," I yelled, jumping out of the chair, breaking off the arms. Her raised eyebrow and the cat hiding behind her skirt, proved otherwise. I growled and threw the pieces of wood at her, but she'd gone by the time they reached the spot she had stood earlier. Storming toward my private chambers, I vowed to teach that little witch some manners. Otherwise, Brian might have to bury her, after all.

I was horny and wanted to fuck someone, but Mary was out of the question, a human from town would be risky since I couldn't drink from them in accord with the rules of the blood moon's Millennial Ball.

"Brian." My voice boomed throughout the empty castle.

"Milord?" He appeared at the still open door like a ghost.

"The blood bag upstairs, is she ready to receive?" The warlock knew well enough what I meant even though I wouldn't say it outright.

"If you don't take too much blood, she's ready." He bowed and disappeared again.

Five seconds later, I was upstairs. Holding my breath, I advanced. With a grimace, I turned the glazed-eyed woman so I wouldn't have to see her face. I closed my eyes and summoned the sight and taste of the girl in the town square. My cock pushed painfully against my trousers. I got rid of all the fabric and crouched on the bed between the woman's legs. Without a thought, I lifted her hips and rammed inside, gritting my teeth at the dry fit. She was too far gone for me to push images in her brain as usual. My cock deflated, and upon a sigh, I got dressed and left the useless blood bag.

I contemplated, for a second, trying to break into the castle to get another taste, but knew it was fruitless. They would be well guarded.

Rubbing a hand over my face, I trudged down the stairs.

"Everything all right, sir?" Brian gazed at me wide-eyed. I never walked. I shrouded and hurried from one place to another.

"I'm not sure." It was the best I could come up with.

Chapter 6 Louisa

When we arrived at the stone monstrosity that was called a castle, the others oh'd and ah'd. I wasn't impressed by its grandeur but rather by the shivers this place gave me. At first I wanted to turn around and run, but the beautiful lady from before welcomed us. When she spoke and clapped her hands, all my dread disappeared.

"Welcome. You are the twenty chosen ones, and will be pampered and fed before the grand ball." She clapped her hands again. "Please follow Karl. He will show you to the bathing area. And most of all, enjoy." As she glided away elegantly, the chatter began again, and we followed Karl as instructed.

The women were separated from the men once we entered a black and white tiled room. Steam rose from sunken tubs that could fit three people. I counted ten, which meant I'd have one all to myself. Not shy, I undressed and sank into the hot water with a sigh. I could live here. This was utter bliss.

A rotund woman wearing a white bathrobe, passed out soap. It smelled of lavender, my favorite scent. I washed my body and hair with soap and hot water, probably for the first time in my life, or at least as long ago as I could remember.

The woman passed again with combs this time.

"Thank you." I stared up at the woman, but she avoided my gaze.

Shrugging, I pulled a comb through my hair for the second time today.

Once I was finished struggling with my hair, I relaxed and soaked up the heat.

I was about to close my eyes, when a new woman came in.

"Ladies, get out and grab yourselves a towel from the pile here. When ready, come to the next room." She left without passing the towels around and our clothes had been removed.

I shrugged and climbed out of the tub, to walk over to the towel rack. Scandalous gasps behind me, got me sniggering. "I'm not going to pass around the towels, so unless you want to turn into a prune, get out."

This got them moving. Without their clothes, they weren't making comments about my body. Everyone had something they were ashamed of. I wasn't ashamed of anything, I liked my body. People came in all sizes, and the assortment getting out of their tubs was no different. I had large boobs, a round bouncy butt, a jelly belly, thick thighs, and all of it was oversized according to people, but I liked them. There were girls behind me that barely reached womanhood and, therefore, had tiny breasts, barely more than nipples.

Another woman had a big butt, but a flat stomach, and hand-sized boobs. One had an hourglass figure, but it was due to wide shoulders and wide hips, not a tiny waist.

Moans filled the air, once the massages began. My masseuse had soft but firm hands. I was still naked, but once the nameless woman held some oil under my nose, prickles spread all over my body. Every touch went deeper and sent me in a daze. Her fingers slipped between my buttocks. A little niggle in the back of my mind tried to push through the haze, but the delicious strokes of her delicate fingers pushed me back into a lull.

The haze over my mind lessened the deeper I went into the castle. Bumping into someone, I apologized and looked up, way up. I read this bulky guy's mind, but wasn't fast enough to react. He grabbed me and forced my hands behind my back. A woman I hadn't seen before approached with an evil smirk. She was dressed all in black leather. Her high heeled boots were covering tight pants with a sleeveless top that barely covered her breasts, finishing the fierce, sexy look. Her skin was as pale as mine. Her black pixie hair was artfully arranged in spikes.

The fierce woman crowded me. I couldn't read her mind, and the glimpse I got from the knife in her hand increased my struggle against the guy's hold.

"Don't worry, little girl, I won't hurt you. Yet." Her evil cackle brought terror alive like I've never felt before. She closed her eyes and inhaled deeply. "Oh, how I love the smell of fear. I'm going to hurt you a little after all. Going to have a little taste." The guy behind me huffed. "Don't worry, brother, It's not like she can tell anyone. Don't you want a taste? Her veins are so pretty and clear." She'd closed in and stroked my neck with a sharp nail.

"Maybe we should bid on her? She's the fattest of them all," she mused.

"Hey, I can hear you." I increased my struggling. "Ouch." Her nail had scraped my neck.

She grabbed my hair and pulled my neck painfully sideways.

"Ew." She was licking my neck with a long stroke of her tongue.

"Mm, savoury. Delicious." Her eyes fluttered in rapture. My face twisted and I tried to control my gag reflex. Disgusting weird people. She still held my neck in the painful position, and with a grunt, the guy behind me sucked the same spot she'd licked. The sucking tightened my nipples.

"Oh," escaped my lips.

Her brother smacked his lips. "Not just savory, sister, but a hint of sweetness. We'll definitely buy this one."

She grinned and before I knew it sliced the knife through the lovely white dress I'd been gifted.

"Oh, my, even though she's fat, she has all the right curves," she muttered and cupped my breasts.

I hummed, which she laughed at. My cheeks heated, and my mind couldn't keep up with how fast my body switched from terror to disgust to enjoyment.

"Let's install her on the podium with a spot in the back," her brother suggested.

"Smart thinking." She nodded.

He picked me up and threw me over his shoulder taking the air out of my lungs. The blurred scenery we passed, hinted at the speed with which they moved. That combined with all my blood rushing to my head, had me passing out.

I came too and lifted my head. When I tried to shield my eyes from the blinding light, my arms were restrained.

"Seriously?" I gasped as I found myself bound to a cross. My wrists were horizontally attached to wooden beams and my ankles to the bottom of a beam that supported my back. The only thing that made sure I was kept aloft and not drooping from my wrists, was a support that protruded between my legs. I was well and truly trussed up. As far as I could crane my neck, I saw a few women and men from the selection, also naked and bound.

I blushed and lowered my gaze when I noticed the members of these men.

Chapter 7 Alexandre

"Mary," I yelled, my voice echoing around the entrance hall.

"I'm here. Hold your horses." She sauntered down the stairs in a light blue dress that barely covered her nipples, but went all the way down to her ankles at least. Her hair was up, not covering anything, and I shook my head when Brian noticed his daughter.

"I put a dress ready for you, and guess what? This wasn't the one," he said in a barely contained voice. He was turning red, and I worried he might have a heart attack.

"Mary, please?" I begged.

"We're late already, so no. I won't change." Her mask in one hand, she kneeled and talked to her cat, petting it.

"You be good now, okay?" she told the cat as if the animal understood her. I shook my head and restrained myself from growling at the beast.

I'd given Mary the wrong time on purpose, since I knew she'd be late. For once, she was on time, making our arrival on the early side. Not that I minded, I wanted another taste of the lovely pale girl. I doubted she still tasted as good as in my imagination. No-one tasted that good. My mind must have been playing tricks on me.

The castle loomed over us when we approached. It didn't look welcoming at all, which I loved and I was sure the humans hated.

I rolled my eyes at the theatrics of the entrance. Flames in torches guided vampires of all sizes, colors, and genders on the way to the ballroom over a cobble stone hallway. The dress code was formal. Having vampires from the new and old world, this ranged from Victorian dresses with ruffles to skimpy skintight dresses. The men wore a black suit with various colors of shirts and ties or bows. My suit was all black, including my shirt. The cufflinks were the only color, rubies. I never cared for bows or ties and as long as it wasn't against Selene's 'rules', I refused to wear them. The colors red and black dominated, with a few purple and green splashes standing out in the throng waiting to enter the ballroom.

Once inside, the usual gothic style candle sconces decorated the walls covered with tapestries. I wondered if they realized the fire hazard. Even living life the old way, I was aware of the stupidity of putting candles near carpets. My eyes widened when I studied the flame of the candle up close. They weren't real. Ah, even Selene couldn't resist adding a bit of new world technology to the ball. Or was it her magic? Shrugging, I folded my hands behind my back. I sauntered among the vamps, greeting a few of the elders, not because I respected them, but of how Selene was always present, and knowing her, waiting to punish someone as entertainment.

I caught the girl's scent a mile away, but couldn't find her. Following my nose, I spotted her at the back of the stage. Good, that way she won't be chosen straight away. Sneaking into her mind, I was surprised at what I found.

Grinning, I approached the stage, but knew that only the high council was allowed on. The guard made sure of that. I would keep an eye on her and coax other interested parties away. It wouldn't be easy, since no-one was allowed to use their powers outright at the ball. Rules again.

Once the ballroom was filled with both high and low born vampires from across the world, either representing their part of the world or per special invitation, the voices overwhelmed me slightly. Not in my own head, but hers. I realised that they used an ointment, weakening her mental blocking system. Her headache was linked to me. Odd, I'd never connected with a human, or a vampire, that much that I took on their pain. I put up my own mental block. It was rusty. I hadn't used it in a long time. Vampires around me knew to block against me, and Brian had put a spell on my blood bags and his mind over the years, allowing me to live freely. I could penetrate the spell, but only if I chose to do that.

Thinking about it, I hadn't had any trouble in the town keeping people's minds closed, unless I concentrated. Maybe I had lost my touch. Seeking out a random human on stage, I listened for his thoughts. They were a jumbled mess, but not through blood loss. It would be impossible. Probably due to the oil. How could I explain the open connection with my pale sassy beauty?

"Something on your mind, son?" My father tapped my shoulder. By the time I turned, he had his hands behind his back as usual. Authority pulsed off his posture, and his sneer was ever present.

"Hello, Mother and Father. How good to see you." The forced smile hurt my face. I didn't offer a hand to my father, but I did hug my mother when she embraced me.

"How are you handling your brother finding his mate? I know it's tough when you haven't found your own," she whispered while keeping me captured in her hug.

"I'm fine, Mother. I don't need a mate." I tried to soften the bite in my voice, but her sigh told me I hadn't succeeded.

"Somehow, I doubt that." She kept me at arms length and peered into my eyes. When hers sparkled with mirth, and she threw her head back laughing, I glared. Father shrugged. My eyes widened as he rolled his eyes and admonished Mother in a calm and caring tone. I hadn't seen them for a few decades, but this change in attitude gave me whiplash. Where was the stern, almost violent father I remembered?

"Well, we have to go. I see Selene approaching the stage, and I don't feel like angering her by not being at her side," Mother mumbled the last part.

Even grumpy vampires can change over time, remember that Alexandre. Mother pushed this thought in my brain, before hurrying to the stage.

Theatrics were never wasted on grandma Selene. Her long hair hung loose around her body, covering her breasts and privates. I thanked my stars for that because the white body hugging dress she wore was see through. We never referred to her as grandma, but my brother and I were direct descendants, as was Barth. None of us, including our parents, wanted to see her fully naked. The demi goddess just couldn't dress properly. Always showing off her figure as if she had to prove something. The woman wouldn't age, ever, why bother proving it?

"Welcome to the blood moon's Millennial Ball. Before we kick off, I'd like to mention that newly turned vampires are to be presented in the next hour. All the servers will be naked and walk among you. Only take a sip here and there, as per usual, otherwise we'll have a very short party." A few chuckles followed that comment.

"We have our stage set up for the tasting. One drop each. As a special treat we have only virgins, even the males." At the many whoops in the crowd. I frowned. I never had a virgin out of fear that she might be my mate.

"Why the special treat? We have two mating ceremonies to complete!" Now a deafening roar and applause hit my eardrums. I pushed my way to the front of the staircase, to make sure I was the first one to taste.

"Let the party begin!" Selene clapped her hands and sparks flew from her fingers to the ceiling, covering it in stars to resemble the current starlit sky outside. Music sounded from nowhere in specific, and the naked servers mingled with the guests.

"Hello, grandmother. This is Mary, my first turned vampire." I bowed and pushed Mary forward, who for once was quivering in fear. She curtsied, and I rolled my eyes when her breasts threatened to spill from her dress.

"Welcome, child. What was the nature of your change?" Her soft voice belied her words. Selene wasn't happy.

"My father is a servant in Lord Alexandre's castle, and when I was on the verge of dying, he asked for me to be turned." At last Mary got up, but kept her eyes lowered. Good girl.

"I see. And how long ago was this?" She raised an eyebrow in my direction and I cringed.

"About nine years." I lifted my chin.

"You know the rules, Alexandre. At least ten years before the blood moon ball and nothing later." She grabbed Mary's chin and raised her head. Mary's wince showed the hard grip Selene had on the girl's chin.

"Are you controlling your urges, girl?" Selene turned Mary's head from side to side.

"Yes, Milady." The girl lied without hesitation. I groaned as Selene smirked.

"Very well. Have fun at the ball." She knew Mary was lying.

"Thank you, Milady." And we hurried away.

I grabbed her arm. "If you make one wrong move, she will kill you. Do you understand." I shook her because she wasn't listening.

"Yeah, yeah." She rolled her eyes.

"I will kill your father if you don't behave, understand?"

Her eyes widened, and she stopped struggling to get away. With a trembling lip she nodded.

Waiting for my turn to taste the naked blood bags bound to crosses, I had to repress my growls every time someone came close to my pale beauty. I was startled when I realised this was the second time I called her 'mine'.

Engulfed in my thoughts, another vampire had to nudge me to move forward. It was almost my turn.

"So, brother, how have you been holding up without fresh blood," came the sarcastic remark from Santos. His very pregnant mate peered up at me, with her hands around her belly. As if she could protect her baby from me. If I wanted the thing dead, even Santos wouldn't be fast enough to stop me. Selene would kill me a second after, though.

"Very good, *brother*. How are you holding up, not being able to drink from your mate?" I laughed aloud, when he grimaced, and his mate's eyes widened.

"Keeping secrets, I see. Let me inform you." I tapped my lips. "You being pregnant means Santos needs to get his blood somewhere else. Being in this part of the world, he can't drink from a bag. Wonder who he's been drinking from?" I winked at her which earned me a scowl and an elbow in Santos' side.

"Don't worry, my dear. Barth has given me blood from, I agree, an unknown and probably living source. But I haven't bitten anyone."

His mate giggled. "Maybe you should bite your brother just in case." They both laughed, but I didn't care, it was my turn. I hurried over to the pale blonde.

Her eyes widened when she recognised me. "Please, choose someone else," she whispered, not knowing I heard her loud and clear.

"I only want you." I pressed my lips on hers, coaxing them apart. My tongue swirled against hers.

Oh my god, he's doing it again. My core is throbbing. Hopefully, he doesn't notice it.

I can smell it, I answered.

"You can hear my thoughts?" Her eyes widened upon the realisation. *Please, say no.*

"Loud and clear." I leaned in and breathed the words against her neck. I recoiled in disgust when I noticed another pair of fang holes.

Kissing my way along her arms, there were marks on her wrists, on her breasts, but not her cunt. *Surely not. He's going to bite me there?*

Kiss you, suck you, drink your juices and have a little taste of blood. She moaned when I showed the images of what I would do, right before I kissed her clit. I had to move her hips forward on the support between her legs to have access to her pussy.

Pressing her fully against my face, I began my feast.

You taste fantastic. I could eat you all day, but unfortunately for now, it'll be a few minutes.

I chuckled before attacking her clit. Sucking it between my fangs gave me the focus I needed for my tongue to lick and flick it.

Faster. She begged.

Hang on, I'm going to bite you now. I wondered for a second why I'd warned her.

My fang pierced her clit enough to draw blood and an agonised scream followed. I grimaced at the pain-filled sound engulfing my brain as well as my ears.

"Don't stop," she begged aloud between pants.

I won't until you soak my face with your juices. I added even more suction, groaning when a droplet of blood shocked my taste buds. She hissed, but the combination of her pain and pleasure-filled blood had me sucking even harder. My cock was straining against my trousers. I flicked my tongue and a long drawn out moan followed by the release of her juices had me right on the edge. The taste of her release was evident in her blood and her pussy. I stopped short when someone tapped me on the shoulder.

"Finished?" It was Santos again, and I rose.

"No," I growled, showing my fangs.

"Wow, dude. Don't worry, I won't bite her." He held up his hands, but the twinkle in his eyes had me take a quick peek into his mind, which surprisingly he allowed.

She's your mate, brother. But don't worry, I'll take her when I get first pick, just to make sure you don't lose her to someone else.

I grabbed him by the throat. "You will do no such thing," I bit out, before releasing him and stomping off the stage.

Chapter 8 Louisa

M*ate?*

"Are you all right?" A very pregnant woman approached me, frowning.

"Of course I'm not fine, you took away the only man that made me feel the best I've ever felt." I blushed furiously, both from admitting this to strangers, and realising it was true. I wanted more. "What did you mean by mate?"

The question widened Alexandre's brother's eyes. "Uh, you read my mind?" He inched closer.

"You can't read mine?" That was ridiculous, he was a vampire.

"No, not everyone can," he chuckled.

"Oh, I thought being a vampire had that perk." I searched for Alexandre's mind, but he was too far away. "So, are you going to bite me, or what?" I was tired of all this talking and ached for the bliss of a minute ago.

"No, we aren't, we're not savages as certain people around here." The chagrin on the woman's face told me it wasn't the norm.

"How do you get blood? As far as I could read minds, it seems like it's your food source."

"We're from a different part of the world and get our blood from volunteers only." He explained.

"What are you doing here then?" I glimpsed a peek into his mind and the picture became clear. "You're forced to be here."

They both nodded. "We'll try and bid on you, so you can choose if you want to go home or Alexandre." The woman, who's name I glimpsed, Caterina, turned to go.

"What's a mate?"

Her eyes widened. "Why would you want to know that?" Caterina asked.

"Because your mate told Alexandre that I was his." I cocked my head and glanced between them.

"Well, it's a vampire's other half, most of the time a human. At least when you're high born." The man pulled his mate closer.

"And Selene decides if you get to have children or not." Caterina grumbled under her breath.

"Really? How does she decide that?"

"By giving you an ultimatum. For us it was, get pregnant in a month or get turned." She smiled at her husband, or mate, whatever.

"We got lucky. The other couple you'll see tonight, wasn't so lucky and she had to be turned or Selene would've killed her." She looked at me with an eyebrow raised.

"She's a real...," I was looking for the word.

Caterina whispered, "Bitch".

"But she's a demi goddess and mother to us all. Nothing to do about it." He shrugged and pulled his wife along.

My mind was overflowing with the information given, but at the same time, I was tired, and dozed off when no-one approached me.

Selene's booming voice startled me awake. "I'm proud to announce the mating of two of my grandchildren."

Applause followed.

"They both had a few weeks time to decide their future and one; Caterina, Santos' mate, is pregnant."

Shouts and whistles ensued.

"They get the second pick of the blood bags in a minute. Our second couple has decided to be changed. Welcome our newest vampire: Michaela!" She was shouting by the end of her announcement, since some decided to whoot before she was finished.

"As a new born, Michaela will choose a blood bag together with her mate."

"We choose the boy on the right." The woman giggled. Even though I'd seen this woman in Caterina's mind, she didn't mind drinking from a human apparently.

"Very well. Caterina, which one do you and your mate choose?" Selene asked.

"The pale one in the back," she told her. I guessed that was me.

"No," Alexandre shouted over the clapping and whistling.

"Alexandre, you'll have to wait your turn." Selene sounded amused.

"They can't have her, she's my, uh, mate." I almost didn't hear the last bit as his voice had reverted from a shout to a near whisper. But the hush falling over the attending crowd, made it clear as day, and my heart skipped a beat.

"Is that so?" Selene drawled.

"Yes," he said a little louder now.

"Well then. Who am I to stand in the way of a mated couple?" Her evil chuckle didn't make her out to be too happy about the whole deal.

"You have three weeks to get her pregnant or she will be dinner for...Patrick." Her triumphant announcement was answered by a roar and some wolf whistles.

Is she for real? This woman was nuts. I needed to get pregnant in three week's time by a stranger, who was also a vampire, or get sucked dry by... Who was Patrick? I didn't care who Patrick was. Did I want to get pregnant? It hadn't been in my plan for the near future. Did I want to get fucked by a smug asshole called Alexandre?

I didn't want that either, but apparently I wasn't asked, my opinion didn't count.

"I guess you'll have to choose another one, Caterina."

She chose the guy next to me, whom I'd been ignoring the whole time. I twisted when a moan to my right caught my attention.

I gaped at the sight. A young woman, barely my age, stroked a man's cock while her mouth sucked at his throat. The man's moans mixed with the girl's hums. My juices flowed freely at the erotic sight, until I noticed his eyes glazed over and his skin paled.

"Stop!" Selene's voice was so loud my ears rang, and she wasn't even in the vicinity.

A blur passed me, and Selene in all her goddess glory appeared. She grabbed the girl by the hair and growled. I trembled in my bindings. The murder in the woman's eyes while looking at the girl was clear as day and crawled over my skin as if it was directed at me next.

Chapter 9 Alexandre

"Oh, Alexandre," Selene sang from the stage. The overwhelming smell of blood on the stage had my fangs bursting free, but dread centered in the bottom of my stomach. Surely Mary wouldn't be that stupid? I hurried up the stage and sure enough, she had Mary by the hair and a male blood bag next to them hung, barely living, from his cross.

"Selene, I'm sorry, I'll take care of it." I rubbed my hand over my face, feeling tired.

"Oh, no, you had your chance. Now it's my turn." The woman put a finger to her mouth as if thinking, but I was sure she had already made up her mind.

"You have your mate, or at least you say she's your mate, but this child of yours will need discipline, and I think a childless couple will be the best case." I held my breath to keep the sigh of relief from escaping. I was sure she was going to kill her, and a warlock going evil on my ass, was not exactly what I'd been waiting for.

She dragged a wide-eyed Mary to the front of the stage. The silence of the attendants of the ball was palpable.

"A special surprise for tonight. All childless couples, please step forward." She waved her hand to beckon them to the front.

"This child needs discipline. She was turned nine years ago." I received a glare from her.

"I'm allowing childless couples to bid on this unruly girl. She's old enough to be disciplined in whichever way you want." Whoots and Selene's evil grin pointed out the sex fact. I wasn't going to tell her that the girl was still a virgin. I winced at Selene's widened eyes.

"I've just been informed that this bad girl is still a virgin. For our pleasure, the winning bid will punish and fuck her on stage. If you're not prepared to do that, refrain from bidding. The money will be awarded to Caterina and Santos for the loss of their choice in blood bag to Alexandre."

The crowd went wild. Mary whimpered and gazed at me. I shrugged and crossed my arms. The pushing of the couples and growls of dominance bored me. I looked at the pale woman and wondered what her name was. I'd have to wait since she passed out after the announcement of the punishment probably.

"Let's start the bidding at—"

"Four thousand," someone called out.

Peering into the crowd, I noticed it was Pierce. The guy's purple hair stood out from the crowd, but not only that, he was a head taller than the rest and twice as wide as my frame. Not an inch of fat on the dude, all muscle. He loved a good fuck, but the petite blonde that was his mate, was a vicious one. Her idea of fun was using the whip wrapped around her waist. I glimpsed the next part of what she planned, and I was surprised. This would be fun.

"Five thousand," someone in the back yelled. Before I found out who it was, six thousand was called out.

"Ten thousand," Pierce called out again, his mate snarling at the couple next to them raising their hand to bid. Knowing her nature, they retracted.

"Fifteen thousand." This time, it was Carly and her mate Baily. Why the hell would they want a girl? A quick glimpse made me grin. They wanted a submissive girl to do their bidding at home, and didn't mind disciplining or fucking her, even if it was with a strap-on.

"Twenty thousand," Samantha, Pierce's mate, called out.

"Twenty-five thousand," Carly shouted.

Pierce bent to whisper to his wife, she nodded.

"Fifty thousand, with a chance for Carly and Baily to have her for one day." Pierce glanced at the pair. They whispered amicably, before turning to Samantha.

"We'll pay you five thousand for a week with the bitch."

Mary gasped when she heard Baily call her a bitch. Carly whispered to Samantha her plans. Apparently it was their anniversary or something, and they hadn't had a submissive in a while.

"Done." Samantha's smile wasn't a pleasant sight, "as long as she doesn't come back without at least a bruise or two. I don't want her to think life is easy." She paused for dramatic effect. "She did after all, almost drain someone at the Millennial Ball."

Mary whimpered and pleaded with her eyes. I shrugged, and turned to see if my pale woman had woken from her slumber.

Slumber, my ass. I fainted, you idiot, and that's a first for me. Knowing I could hear her thoughts, her eyes sparkled with fire. *Now get me off this cross, Mate.*

But you look so pretty, all bound and vulnerable. I pouted.

Your testicles would also look pretty all bound and vulnerable. She cocked her head, fluttering her eyes. I threw my head back and laughed, earning me a glare from Selene.

"Before we start the punishment, I'd like all couples to choose their blood bag, and get them off the stage." Selene dragged Mary by the hair.

The couples stood in line awaiting their turn. The line formed according to ranking, while I approached my woman.

Tearing the rope with my nails, she fell into my arms. I crouched to release her ankles, letting her glide across my shoulder. When I stood, I grabbed her ass to keep her luscious body from slipping to the floor. She grumbled something under her breath, and I spanked her bountiful behind with a resounding slap.

"You..." I stopped her before she could insult myself and anyone in hearing distance.

Careful there, words and actions get you killed here.

She stilled, but I couldn't resist squeezing her buttocks. My palms overflowed with her soft cheeks. I couldn't wait to bury my cock between them.

But, first things first. We were to attend the punishment of my stupid vampire creation.

Chairs were brought in by the servers, at least the ones that were able. One male was occupied. Corpius pounded away in the young human's ass. The blood bag had his hands against a pillar whimpering and squeezing his eyes shut at every thrust. Corpius grabbed the guy's hair to pull his back flush with his chest. His fangs penetrated the boy's neck, holding him there while he kept pumping. His hands, now free again, grabbed onto his hips, his thrusts increasing in speed. His fangs kept the guy aloft. Francine passed them and stopped to admire the beauty of it all. She grabbed the boy's cock and pumped it as fast as Corpius' s thrusts. Leaning in, she opened her mouth and her fangs sank into his chest, covering a nipple. When the boy came all over her hand, Corpius stopped moving and grunted. Both him and Francine let go of the boy and licked the wounds to close them.

"Take your seats, please, and let the show begin." Selene's voice quieted the crowd.

I found a seat not too far from the stage, wanting a close view for myself and the woman I draped over my lap.

Chapter 10 Louisa

His arms tightened around my waist when I wriggled to get more comfortable. My arms felt like ants were crawling over them, now that blood was rushing back into them.

Sit still, or I'll open my trousers and put my cock where I want it to be.

I gasped. When I tried to turn my head, he whispered in my ear, "Pay attention to the stage. This is what happens when Selene isn't happy."

In front of us, the raised daise had been cleared of all the crosses, erasing the fact that humans, myself included, had been strung up like cattle to be tasted and prodded.

A table was placed in the center, and the cute girl that had been sucking and pleasuring the guy next to me, was draped over it. We were so close, I saw her naked body trembling and tears formed in her eyes.

"Why aren't you helping her? She's yours, is she not?" I whispered to the man holding my wrists in one hand and stroking my thigh with the other.

"She needs punishment for her deeds, and this is better than death, don't you think?"

I wasn't so sure about that.

Her arms were stretched across the table. A giant man attached two pieces of rope to her wrists, binding them together.

He dragged the rest of the rope under the table to her ankles. One rope per ankle bound her to the legs of the table.

Can't she break the rope? From what I saw so far, they were all strong, and fast.

No, we use this rope rarely, but I guess Pierce bought it from a jailor. It's used to restrain vampires before sentencing them.

A tiny woman dressed fully in leather, similar to the garb I'd seen before, sauntered onto the stage, cracking a bullwhip as she closed in on the table. *Holy crap! She's going to use that on her?*

We heal fast, but it's still going to hurt. Alexandre licked my ear and a shiver ran down my spine. The man was lethal with his mouth. I concentrated on closing my mind to his. A reverse boundary of sorts. I had to try, I didn't want him to read my every thought. I jumped and opened my eyes when a crack of the whip connected with skin, and Mary screamed bloody murder.

The whole crowd hushed. Two moans came from the back of the room. I twisted and this time Alexandre let me.

A server had her mouth over a man's penis. His hand was fisted in her hair, and he used it to pull and push her head up and down. Next to him sat a woman with her skirt around her waist, her pussy bare for all to see. She stroked it with her fingers, her gaze riveted on the stage.

The next scream brought my attention to the scene on stage.

Blood from the two lashes splattered the crowd when the woman brought the whip over her head, which had some muttering and others smacking their lips. I shivered in disgust.

Four more vicious cuts by the whip ended the punishment. The sweat soaked girl slumped in her bounds as much as she could.

Not realising I'd held my breath, I released it on a whoosh.

The man approached his mate, grabbed her hair and twisted her head backward, before bending himself to devour her mouth. I squeezed my thighs together to ease the ache there, but was hindered by a hand.

"Open," Alexandre growled. I opened my legs, hoping his hand would travel towards my nub and bring me to orgasm again.

"Put your hands on your head," was his next request. This position gave him full access, but I wouldn't deny myself the pleasure I found with him before, just because I was naked. I was beyond caring about that.

On stage, the man took off his trousers and a snake as thick as my wrist came out. A gasp escaped my lips.

"Don't worry, mine isn't nearly as big as that," Alexandre chuckled.

I bit my lower lip and watched the thing approach Mary from behind.

His mate opened Mary's pussy lips, eliciting a moan from the girl. She was writhing on the table, almost humping it.

"Oh, she wants it all right," a guy next to us said who was stroking his cock.

I blushed and turned to the stage again, where the woman guided her mate's cock into the girl's pussy.

A hand clasped over my own and pressed into it. When Alexandre pushed his fingers in and used his palm to rub my nub, I was in seventh heaven. At least I thought I was. Pierce had the tip of his huge thing inside the girl's pussy. He bent forward and grabbed the top of the table, dwarfing the little girl. With a grunt, he pushed forward. I winced together with the girl. That couldn't feel good.

Read her mind. Alexandre kept a slow rotation over my nub, but didn't do anything else.

Opening my mind to the naked girl, I gasped.

Come on, move already. I need him to move. Move it, damn it. He's so deep. So deliciously deep.

"Please," the girl begged.

"What?" the guy asked with gritted teeth.

"Fuck me." She squealed as he moved, slowly.

Faster, you dumbwit. I grinned at her mental debate.

He did move faster, and her pleasure washed over to me. Alexandre moved his fingers in and out at the same time with Pierce's strokes.

Grab my, ooh yes, dig those thick fingers in them, rip them open. Oh my, so close, so close.

I gaped. He was digging his fingers in her shoulders and pressing his thumbs into the scars scabbing over from the whipping. And she begged him to open them up?

His mate came closer and dug her nails into the girl's back dragging them from butt to shoulders. Mary screamed, and in my mind, her orgasm slammed into me.

I rotated my hips searching for the same thing.

"Fuck, she's coming," Pierce gritted between his teeth. His rhythm became erratic right before he shuddered and kissed his mate leaning over the table, burying his cock deep inside the girl who'd passed out. When he pulled out his semen dripped out of her pussy.

I closed my eyes since Alexandre was using his hands to finger my nub and pump into my soaked pussy. Next thing I knew, he bit my shoulder, and I saw stars, shuddering all over, clamping my thighs around his hands. He licked my neck and lifted me. I moaned, he took away the aftershock pleasure. That was twice now that my orgasm was cut short. Knowing from self pleasuring, I was aware of the bliss that came after an orgasm.

He grabbed me again and lifted me over his shoulder.

"I'd advise you to close your eyes," he warned me.

"Why?" But he didn't answer my question, and the world blurred around me. I was quick to close my eyes before my stomach could expel the little content it still had inside.

Chapter 11 Alexandre

I threw her onto my bed. Now that I had her here, I wasn't sure what to do. The girl curled into a ball, all the sass leaving her. Round eyes watched my every move.

Her mind ran a million miles per hour, and I couldn't quite catch her thoughts. Her smell told me she was petrified. I wanted to suck her delicious blood and fuck until she couldn't walk straight. So what was keeping me?

Brian was cooking, and the hideous smell assaulted my senses.

A moan drew me out of my thoughts. She inhaled deeply, and with closed eyes, she hummed her delight.

"Hungry?" I smirked, and her eyes shot open wide, before squinting.

Her only answer was a nod.

"What would you do for some food, I wonder?" I focused on her thoughts.

Right now, I would kill. Preferably you.

I threw my head back and laughed.

"Everything all right?" Brian asked from the open door.

She scrambled back into a ball trying to hide her beautiful assets.

"My blood bag is hungry." When I grinned, Brian raised an eyebrow. Even though he blocked his thoughts, I read them clearly on his face: *What the hell?*

"Good, I made enough stew for two. Will Mary be back soon?" he asked while turning to go downstairs to the kitchen.

I winced and glared at the woman on my bed. *You don't want to know what I'll do to you if you say anything.* As she opened her mouth, I pushed a scenario where I whipped her until she bled and licked the blood from the wounds. She snapped her mouth closed.

"Would you have some clothes or should I wrap the blanket around myself?" She was already doing that the moment Brian left.

"I'll see what I can find," I sighed. Mary's clothes wouldn't fit her, and it wasn't as if I had women's clothes laying around.

"Check that drawer there, there should be a shirt that would cover you." I pointed. When she didn't move, I raised an eyebrow.

"Go away, so I can change." *And maybe find an escape route.*

I shook my head. *Not going to happen, sweetheart.*

With an outraged shriek, she dropped the blanket and ran to the drawer. The first shirt she grabbed was one of my favorites. A black button down silk shirt. It reached her knees in the front. She tried to pull it lower in the back, to cover her voluptuous ass. I was glad that my shirts weren't overly long. She had to make a choice, back or front.

"Come on." I turned to hide the smirk, when she still pulled on the front and the back, trying in vain to cover everything at once.

Her humming during dinner had me on edge. I hated the smell of human food, but if it made her heart rate thrum and her blood soar, I'd struggle through it. Except for the uncomfortable fit of my trousers, I'd endure anything that made her happy.

The thought was so absurd that I left the table.

When I heard Brian ask about Mary, I hurried back and picked the woman up.

"I wasn't finished," she squealed.

"I'll give you something else to suck on." That shut her up, but also aroused her. Pleasantly surprised, I threw her onto the bed for the second time tonight.

After ridding myself of my clothes, I pulled her legs to the edge of the mattress and over my shoulders. When she struggled, I nipped her calf. On a gasp, she stilled.

I touched her pussy to make sure she was wet for me. She wasn't as wet as before, but I couldn't wait anymore. With one delicious thrust I entered her. She was tight and screamed. Frowning, I pulled back. The fact she was a virgin no more, showed in the blood covering the tip of my cock.

Growling in satisfaction of being the first one to have her, I thrust in again, pumping my cock inside as fast and as deep as I could. I bent her legs further so I could reach her nipples. So far she hadn't reacted, but the pinch woke her. A ripple inside caressed my cock. I slowed down, savoring the feeling. When I opened my eyes, I gazed at her and the tears on her cheeks. I let her legs fall from my shoulders and descended my mouth to her lush lips. When I nipped them, she opened up and a moan escaped us when our tongues caressed. I hadn't moved since I saw her tears and was baffled by my emotions. Since when did I care if I hurt a blood bag?

When she lifted her hips, I pulled out to the tip and slammed back home. A slow leisurely rhythm had her frowning. She tried to move her hips, but was trapped. Only my elbows next to her body kept me from crushing her completely.

"Tell me what you want?" I knew but wanted her to admit it aloud. I grinned as her frown deepened, but her eyes remained shut.

I pulled out again, gritting my teeth, since it was getting harder to go slow. When I rammed in hard and fast, her eyes opened wide.

"Is that what you want?" I repeated the thrust.

"Oh," she moaned and closed her eyes. She arched her back, pushing her breasts into my chest.

"Tell me," I gritted out. She narrowed her eyes at me and wrapped her hands around my ass, touching me for the first time.

"Tell me," I demanded. Instead, she dug her nails into my ass, but I wasn't going down that easy. I stopped moving completely.

"No," she begged.

"What?" I propped my head on my hands and kept still.

"Move," she tried to command me and wiggled her hips.

"Not good enough. Tell. Me. What. You. Want." I bit my lip, showing my fangs. Her hands caressed my back, never taking her gaze off my mouth.

"I want you to fuck me and bite me," she whispered, but that was good enough for me.

Grabbing her wrists, I pushed them into the mattress next to her head. I planted my feet into the carpet and started a rhythm that literally took her breath away. She thrashed under me, putting her feet on the edge of the mattress to push back, but I was moving too fast. When her pussy clamped down on my cock, I released her wrists and grabbed a handful of hair. Twisting her head sideways, I sank my teeth into her soft neck, just as the walls of her pussy spasmed around my cock, massaging it. The taste of her blood and the feel of her orgasming, threw me over the edge. When I licked her wounds, I noticed she'd passed out. I grinned, pretty pleased with myself for not having to use compulsion at all to get a human off.

Chapter 12 Louisa

I came to in a soft bed with a thick duvet covering my naked body. When I stretched, I grinned at the complaining muscles I had never used before. I slid my hands under the duvet and caressed my sensitive body. My nipples tightened the moment I touched them. When I reached my pussy, I glanced around the room. Not seeing Alexandre, I opened it and gently tapped my clit before lazily circling it. My eyes fluttered closed, and I rubbed my nub faster. With my other hand, I covered my mouth to silence the moans trying to escape. I arched my back, and the soft fabric covering me caressed my nipples.

"Hey," I squealed as the duvet was pulled from me.

"That pussy is mine," Alexandre growled, looming over the side of the bed. I still had my fingers on my pussy and seeing him, my cheeks flamed hot. Keeping eye contact, I started rubbing again, daring him to stop me.

His eyes narrowed.

Do you want me to throw you over my lap?

The visual thought creeped into my mind, and I rubbed faster. It confused and aroused me that I wanted him to spank me.

A whoosh of air was all the warning I had before his hand connected with my ass. He'd manoeuvred me over his legs on the side of the bed. The blood rushed into my head, and my pussy moistened even further. My moans and squeals became louder with each slap.

Another whoosh of air, had me with my back against a wall. I wrapped my legs around his waist and my arms around his neck. He shook his head, and I dropped them to the side, palms pressed against the wall next to my ass.

In one smooth stroke, he entered me. This must be what heaven was like. I threw my head back, banging it into the wall. He started a pace that was humanly impossible, I was sure of it, banging my back into the wall with every thrust.

"Yes, yes, yes," I chanted. Even dazed with pleasure, I still read his confused thoughts.

How am I going to get her to drink my blood and accept me as her mate? I'm not even sure she is my mate, but we won't know until we do that. I wish I could just fuck her for the rest of eternity.

That last bit made me smile, and I couldn't focus on the first part as I was losing all thoughts of my own, let alone his.

He let one of my legs drop to the floor. On my tip toes, I winced when he pulled my other leg into the air. I wasn't that flexible. I tried to push him away, but was dazzled when he bit my calf. All aches focused on the pain and pleasure of his bite. This position gave my nub full contact with his groin, and after four strokes, I was on the edge.

He'd dropped my leg, taking my orgasm away.

"No," I screamed.

An evil grin greeted me when I glared at him. He twisted me around and put my hands against the wall. Pushing into me again, I sighed in contentment. I wanted to squeeze my breast and pinch my nipple. He did it for me the second the thought entered my mind, and I hummed in delight. Trying that again, I imagined his hand on my nub rubbing it just the right way.

His chuckle made me grin. He realised what I was doing, but his hand traveled over my belly to my clit anyway. He only needed to rub it a few times, and I tightened. His cock pumped through my tightening muscles, repeatedly hitting a soft spot that brought me closer.

Covering each breast with a hand, he hugged me against his hard chest. He didn't stop pumping into me, and didn't stop pushing back, as much as I could. I froze when his hands moved to my neck and lightly circled it, using the leverage to push me backwards against his cock. My hands moved frantically and held onto his, frightened he might tighten them. To my utter relief, he put them on my shoulders instead. I dropped my hands again, and let my head fall onto his shoulder. He took the invitation it was and bit down hard. I went over the edge, screaming my release, going limp in his arms.

I frowned when he pulled out and picked me up to put me under the covers again.

"What about you?" I asked an empty room. He'd already left.

The next time I woke, it was to the smell of freshly baked bread and a grumbling tummy. Jumping out of bed, I shrugged into the shirt Alexandre gave me yesterday and hurried barefoot to the kitchen.

"Good morning, miss," Brian greeted with a sad smile.

"Good morning. What's wrong?" I asked. I was hesitant to read his mind. His aura almost pushed me before I even tried.

"Alexandre told me about Mary yesterday. It's all my fault." The old man stopped cutting the cheese, and hung his head.

I took a small step closer, and rubbed his back.

"I don't think her lack of restraint is your fault." I'd learned from Mary's own mind, that she hadn't believed it herself. She'd been berating herself the whole time childless couples were bidding on her.

"I was the one that insisted on Alexandre changing her, even though it was within the timeframe of the blood moon ball." He slammed his fist on the cutting board, making me jump.

"Did he tell Mary the risks?" I wrung my hands. Surely Alexandre wasn't so callous as to change a girl against the bitch of a demi goddess?

"We both did, but she's my little girl, you know. And she didn't have another nine years left." His shoulders shook. On a sniff, he raised his head, and picked up the knife. "Well, it's done now. Nothing to do about it." He shook his head and continued cutting.

"At least she's still alive," I mumbled.

"I'm not sure if that's a good or a bad thing," he said more to himself than me.

"I saw her last night, and she did get punished, but was quite happy when she left with that couple," I assured him.

He turned with the knife in my direction, his eyes widened. "Are you sure?"

"Y-yes, I-I'm s-sure." I didn't take my eyes off the knife, an inch from my chest.

"Oh, I'm sorry." He put down the knife and glanced at me sheepishly. "How do you know she was happy?"

"I can read minds when they are open to me." I shrugged.

He crossed his arms and peered into my eyes. When he nodded and turned to the cutting board, I wondered what just happened.

"Thank you. I wish Alexandre had told me, instead of letting me think the worst." He went back to cutting.

I grabbed a glass of water and sat at the table patiently waiting for him to finish the cheese and jam bread slices.

While I licked my fingers, the back door creaked open. I nearly choked on the last piece of bread when a cat the size of a small cow entered the kitchen. Brian chuckled.

Never taking my eyes off the animal, who cocked it's head and stared straight back, I asked: "What's this?"

"It's, or rather was, Mary's pet leopard, Princess."

The leopard's ears perked, and she approached Brian, who petted her and gave her some cheese.

"She's a pet?" I was watching the pair astonished at the trust both human and animal had in each other.

"She raised her from a cub when she was still human."

The leopard put her head on his lap and purred up a storm.

"She's gorgeous," I whispered in awe of the magnificent beast.

"Don't run," Brian warned me, and before I could wonder why, Princess approached me. She put her paws on my bare legs, without claws piercing my skin. I sat dead still, not moving an inch as the cat's nose closed in on mine, until I looked cross-eyed.

A purr gave me shivers, when it was followed by a lick, I giggled. Her tongue was rough, scraping my face. Releasing my fear, I scratched her behind the ear, and her purr grew louder, almost deafeningly so. Every time I stopped scratching, she nudged my hand with her head. I wasn't frightened, but still wasn't going to ignore her demands. I had a slight suspicion she knew it.

Chapter 13 Alexandre

I woke up to a deadly silence. Searching the house for a heartbeat, I only found Brian's. In a panic, I rushed downstairs, rubbing the spot where my heart used to be. It felt emptier than before.

"Where is she?" I roared.

"I sent your blood bag to the people currently housing my daughter." Brian's eyes blazed, and I took a step back. An angry warlock with his power could harm me with a snap of his fingers.

"I don't mean the blood bag, my...uh." Laughter interrupted my babbling.

"You mean, Louisa?" Brian wiped the tears from his eyes.

"Yes. Her. My mate." I smirked when Brian gaped.

"You've got to be kidding me. That wonderful sweet girl is your mate? What were the fates thinking?" He threw his hands up and kept mumbling. When he turned, my patience snapped.

"Where is she?" I barked.

"You should be able to sense her general whereabouts. Why can't you?" The old man narrowed his eyes. "You aren't officially mated yet, are you?"

"I'm getting tired of your questions. Tell me where she is, or I'll..." I shook my head. There wasn't anything I could do to the man. Maybe withhold my blood, but he wouldn't care now that his daughter was somewhere else.

"She's at the lake," Brian informed me before returning to whatever he was cooking.

"Ah, hell, no," I muttered when I closed in on my mate playing in the water, naked, with Mary's cat.

I watched from behind a tree when the moonlight hit her pale breasts and stomach as she floated in the water. The cat was on the grass glaring my way. I hissed which she reciprocated.

"What's wrong, princess?" My mate came out of the water and dressed in my shirt, while nervously checking her surroundings. "Maybe we should head back home?" She caressed the feline and it purred. The creature's head reached her waist. Her hand never left its head. When they approached the tree I was hiding behind, the stupid cat pushed her in another direction.

Pissed off, I ran into the house, pacing in front of the fireplace.

"You're awake," she greeted me wearily.

"What? No good morning?" I smirked, leaning against the stones. She shivered, but it wasn't in fright.

"It's not like I can say 'good morning' when it's evening." She hugged herself.

"Brian, can you light the fireplace, please?" I called out without moving from my spot against the wall. We stared at each other, but our minds were closed.

Once the fire was lit, she crouched in front of it. "We have to talk," she stated, gazing into the flickering flames.

"I know." I rubbed a hand over my face and sat in the nearest chair.

"As far as I can tell, just having sex won't get me pregnant."

I raised an eyebrow at her back. "Who told you that?"

"I may have peeked into Caterina's mind when she talked about mates." Louisa turned to cheekily smile at me.

"Yeah, you have to accept me as your mate and drink blood from me." It remained dead quiet.

She'd scrunched up her nose at the drinking blood, but was thinking it over.

When she smiled, I sighed in relief, until I noticed it was that stupid cat sauntering in as if she owned the place.

"And the cat has to go," I growled.

She ignored me and hugged the giant beast as if it were a kitty cat. "The big bad man doesn't mean it," she told the cat while squishing its face. "You don't mean it, right?" She raised an eyebrow. "Mate of mine." Her smile widened when I gasped, and I could swear my dead heart thumped once.

"You mean it? You accept me as your mate?" As I asked the question, she sashayed my way. She put her hands on the chair and descended slowly. Her breasts swayed loosely under my shirt. When she bent, I could see her whole body, but the sparkle in her eyes interested me more. Such joy and naughtiness were captured there.

She gave me a peck on the cheek but didn't stop there. Her plump lips kissed a path down my jaw, until she nipped my neck, startling me. She giggled and tried to run off, but I grabbed her around the waist and drew her body close to mine. She landed awkwardly on my lap with flailing limbs. I laughed at her giggles filling the empty castle. When she sobered, she pulled my head down. Our lips touched, and on a moan, we opened up to each other, tongues duelling. She tried to crawl closer, pulling herself up so she could straddle my lap. I grabbed her ample buttocks and squeezed, bringing her bare pussy in contact with my trousers. She ground herself onto my covered cock.

"I need your blood and cock now," she whimpered, trying to press her body closer, but getting frustrated with our clothes. She ripped my shirt off her body and feverishly unbuttoned my fly. I lifted my hips to help her, curious as to how far she'd take this.

Grabbing my cock in one hand, she put the other on my shoulder and lifted on shaking thighs. She positioned the head at her entrance and sank down ever so slowly. We both groaned. I leaned back in the chair, and she followed, burying her face in the crook of my neck. She set a slow pace, rubbing her clit onto my abdomen on every downward stroke. When she suckled my neck, I nearly lost it.

Lighting fast, I grabbed her hair and kissed her deeper than before, conquering her mouth. I let go, slashed my nail into the skin in my neck and guided her face there.

When she sucked, at first, it was hesitant, but every increase in suction, I felt all the way to my dick. Grabbing her hips, I took over the rhythm, and when she threw her head back, I attacked her beautiful taught nipples, piercing them like I had her clit at the ball. She screamed, but it was in ecstasy as I was sucked as hard as she had before. When her orgasm ripped through her, her muscles massaged me. She slumped down, my cock still buried deep in her.

Chapter 14 Louisa

I stirred when his cock grew inside me. My head snapped up.

"Wha...?" My question ended in a scream, tears gathering in my eyes.

"Fuck," he groaned. His cock kept swelling and going deeper, without either of us moving.

I tried to get off his lap, but upon a cry, and his grimace, I stayed. I buried my face in his neck and whimpered.

"I'm sorry," he mumbled in my neck, before biting down hard. I let myself feel that familiar pain, trying to ignore the fact that his cock was breaching another barrier. He worried my neck with his teeth, and an orgasm ripped through me so fast and hard, I fainted.

I woke up covered in a blanket on the sofa.

"It's normal? Are you kidding me? How can it be normal to hurt a mate?" Alexandre paced in front of the fireplace holding a black brick to his ear. "Santos, how am I going to do this again? I couldn't take the pain away," anguish was clear in his voice. He slammed his fist into the wall, leaving a dent in the stone. "And did it happen again with you?" He chuckled but it lacked warmth. "Right. Keep trying." He threw the black brick onto a nearby table, cursing Selene.

I sat up, gathering the blanket around me. His gaze settled on me, spiking a shiver. In a flash, he pulled me into his arms, onto his lap, and buried his nose in my hair"I'm...sorry. How are you feeling?" he asked as if it was normal to have a conversation with a brick.

"I'm fine, are you okay?" I gestured to the table.

He frowned then laughed. "It's a phone. Something from the modern world to speak to people over a long distance. Brian made it work in these parts last night." As if that explained anything.

"So, you 'spoke' to Santos about..." I gestured between us, feeling the heat crawl up my face.

"It's normal between mates when one is still human and means that we could be pregnant."

"Is it going to happen every time?" I shivered involuntarily. I wasn't sure if I could handle that much pain on a regular basis.

He grimaced. "It depends on if you're pregnant or not. As long as you're not pregnant, it will happen again." He sighed.

I nodded, and my stomach rumbled, reminding me it had been quite a while since my last meal.

"Let's see what Brian cooked for you." Alexandre stood and held out his hand.

I took it once I realized I was dressed in his shirt again.

"CAN I SPEAK WITH CATERINA on that...thing?" I asked after dinner.

"It's a phone, but yes, you can." Alexandre yawned and dragged me away from the table. "I think it's time to go to bed."

"I'm not ready to have sex again right now." I tried to pull my hand from his.

"It's time for bed, I'll be passed out in an hour and want to get comfortable," he explained.

"The sun is about to rise, why go to bed?" I frowned.

"Because he's a vampire, my dear. And vampires burn to a crisp in the sun," Selene said in all her sugar sweet voice.

"Ouch." Alexandre was squeezing my hand.

"Sorry," he mumbled, never taking his eyes off Selene. "How dare you come here?" he growled.

"Excuse me? I can come and go wherever and whenever I please." She raised her chin glaring at him.

"Because of you, I have to hurt my mate to get her pregnant. If I could kill you and lift this curse, I would." He took a step forward, but I hugged his arm, which calmed him a smidgen.

"Everything all right, Lord A..." Brian stared at the goddess, his mouth hanging wide open.

"Brian, Selene. Selene, Brian." Alexandre introduced the two. "And no, everything is not all right," he gritted between his teeth.

"She ordered me to get Louisa pregnant or she'd have her killed." His voice broke, but neither reacted. I glanced from Brian to Selene. They hadn't taken their attention off each other.

Has Selene ever had a mate? I questioned Alexandre.

He raised an eyebrow. *No. She created us because she couldn't find her mate and wanted children.*

Watch them. I grinned, knowing I was right.

I peeked into Selene's mind, careful not to alert her. The only thoughts I picked up were unbelief and mate.

"You've got to be kidding me." Alexandre's eyes widened. I laughed aloud until Selene pinned me with a glare. Lowering my gaze, I allowed Alexandre to tug me against him.

"We'll continue this discussion tomorrow," Selene said.

"What discussion?" I was confused. She never actually told us why she showed up.

"Him cursing me." She pointed at Alexandre, who tightened his arms around me.

Before anyone could say another thing, she disappeared, taking Brian with her.

Alexandre carried me to bed. He crawled in and pulled me close. His cock pressed into my lower back and his hand held one of my boobs. I snuggled closer, and his grip tightened.

"Careful," he whispered.

"Why?" I asked breathlessly. I squeezed my legs together when his cock grew.

"Because, if we start, I won't be able to stop, and I don't want to hurt you again." He kissed my ear.

"Are we never having sex again because you don't like to hurt me?" I turned in his arms.

"Definitely not what I'm saying."

I giggled when he tickled me. I flipped him onto his back, straddling his waist. He let me, he was after all stronger than myself.

"Now what?" He put his arms under his head and raised an eyebrow.

"Now, I devour you." My chuckle turned into a moan when he pulled me down for a toe curling kiss.

"Are you sure?" He searched my eyes.

I nodded, heat crawling over my skin from his intense gaze and protectiveness.

"Just make sure you bite me before you...uh...grow." My whole body was on fire. I needed his hands, his lips, his fangs, and his cock.

He tried to slow me down, but I was having none of it, grabbing his wrists and pushing them into the mattress. My hips gyrated against his cover-clad cock as I sucked his earlobe. He groaned, which made me smile. I wanted him as needy as I was.

Sitting up, I took his hands with me and pressed them to my breasts. Still moving, my clit was in contact with the fabric. Sweat beaded on my upper lip, and I frowned, searching for my release. It was just out of reach. So close. Alexandre pinched my nipples, and I cried out, opening my eyes

"Why? I was so close," I moaned.

Fast as lighting, he changed our position. His fingers explored my soaking pussy, and pressed a thumb hard onto my clit. All of his actions brought me to the edge of orgasm, but never over. When I glared at him, his knowing grin greeted me back.

In one swift move, he entered all the way. I writhed beneath him, knowing that with a little friction, I would be flying. He kept my orgasm on hold. When I sneakily tried to move my hands between our bodies, he growled and grabbed them both, pushing them above my head.

With every thrust, I pushed back as much as I could. A salty flavor entered my mouth when I bit my lip and whimpered. That's when he bit my neck. I froze and tightened my inner muscles around his cock involuntarily, before a shuddering orgasm broke through. My cries were accompanied by his growl in my neck. His cock pulsed inside, extending my orgasm. When I relaxed again, I opened my eyes to a tender smile.

"Aren't you going to...?" I gestured to his cock.

"I already did."

I frowned, it hadn't hurt this time. I gazed at my mate in wonder.

"Are we...?

"Pregnant? I think so." His jubilant smile could've lit up a room.

I'm pregnant. My hand caressed my tummy. He dropped on his side and covered my hand with his, kissing my shoulder. Pulling me closer, we fell asleep peacefully in the knowledge of our luck.

"I GUESS I WON'T HAVE to kill you after all. Ugh, now I owe Patrick another blood bag." Selene popped in muttering the last part.

"Could you please announce your arrival next time? I might die of a heart attack." I rubbed the spot where my heart was doing overtime.

"I'm a busy woman. I don't have time for that." She lifted her chin.

"Busy with Brian?" Alexandre smirked.

I gaped when the cool demi goddess blushed.

"I wanted to congratulate you both, and I'll be keeping Brian."

Alexandre and I exchanged an amused glance.

"For compensation, of course." She glared at Alexandre.

"Of course." He grinned back.

She disappeared, and we laughed until tears ran down our cheeks.

"I'm going to talk to Caterina and tell her," I told Alexandre, holding out my hand for the brick.

"She's never going to believe it!"

63

Author's note

Thank you so much for reading this final story in the current Vampire story. I hope you liked it!

If you have a few minutes to leave a review, I would appreciate it immensely!

About the Author

Tiny Sparks is the nom the plume of an author of erotic and romantic short stories.

Her husband and their special relationship are the inspiration for her erotic short stories. She is his submissive and therefore has experience in the BDSM scene.

When she could not find enough stories to satisfy her, she decided to write her own.

Some stories offer sexy fantasies with a personal knowledge of the BDSM world. Other stories are more in the paranormal or fantasy genre.

Other books by Tiny Sparks
Riding red Werewolf Erotic Story

After finding a stranger in her grandma's house, Red soon learns about the debt she must settle. There's no way around it but to barter herself. However, what's required isn't the usual sort of work. Within the den of her sworn enemies, she has to swallow her pride and serve the pack males.

18+ erotic scenes, only loosely based on the fairy tale Red Riding Hood, werewolves

https://books2read.com/u/mV6ro2

Initiation BDSM Erotic Stories : Book 1

Tina has a fabulous imagination, giving her the opportunity to write sexy articles for a magazine. When offered a full time writer's gig, she's all for it.

This time, however, her imagination won't help her as they want a personal touch. A colleague at her current job might just give her all the experience she needs, and more. How far will she go to become a full time writer?

https://books2read.com/u/b6Ok5Z

Introduction BDSM Erotic Stories
Book 2

Book 2 in the BDSM Erotic Stories series

Tina's research is going well in theory. Barry keeps offering delicious information in regards to extending her BDSM experience. She gladly takes him up on it and will soon find out how far she will go to squeeze out the maximum pleasure from all the wonderful new impressions. However, her relationship with Barry is still a question mark. He doesn't hint at being more than her tutor and temporary Dom and she doesn't ask.

https://books2read.com/u/3k5pa6

Invitation BDSM Erotic Stories Book 3

Book 3 in the BDSM Erotic Stories

As their relationship blossoms, Tina and Barry explore BDSM further. When a revelation pops up, Barry is excited but Tina doesn't know what to think.

Follow these two in the third book of the series.

https://books2read.com/u/3ye1NL

!Stalk me!

Newsletter
https://landing.mailerlite.com/webforms/landing/f7o1s4

Twitter
https://www.twitter.com/SparksxTiny
Facebook
https://www.facebook.com/tiny.sparksx.73
Instagram
https://www.instagram.com/sparksxtiny/
Website
http://www.tinysparksx.wixsite.com/tinysparks